A TREASURY OF TALES

TAHIR SHAH

YAROSLAVA MOROSOVA

A TREASURY OF TALES

TAHIR SHAH

YAROSLAVA MOROSOVA

MMXXIII

Secretum Mundi Publishing Ltd
124 City Road
London
EC1V 2NX
United Kingdom

www.secretum-mundi.com
info@secretum-mundi.com

First published by Secretum Mundi Publishing Ltd in
Daydreams of an Octopus & Other Stories, 2022
Published in this edition, 2023

A TREASURY OF TALES

Artwork drawn by Yaroslava Morosova

A CIP catalogue record for this title is available from the British Library.

ISBN 978-1-914960-88-8

VERSION 21112022

Visit the author's website:
Tahirshah.com

Once upon a time,
in the distant reaches of the East,
a young man named Zaliak had a dream.

He dreamt that every single story in the world
was collected together in a great treasury,
a repository to match the treasure troves
of gold so protected and admired in
the kingdom's capital.

As a child, Zaliak had learned that there were two different kinds of dream…

The first kind was amusing,
and amusing alone.

Filling heads through long winter nights, they had little or no bearing on decisions, destiny, or on anything else.

The second kind of dream was altogether different.

As amusing as the first kind, they held an extraordinary power – a power to chart the twists and turns of fate.

Waking from his slumber, Zaliak wiped his eyes. Then, sitting up, he knew at once that the dream he had just experienced was one which reflected Providence.

Without wasting a moment, the young man dressed, then considered what to do. The answer was in his mind even before the question had been conjured.

He would seek out the one person alive who had an answer for every question: the Wise Man of Slew, who lived in the forest beyond the Slaked Grey Mountains.

So, taking a little bread and a handful of dates, he set off in search of an answer to the meaning of his dream.

For days and nights, Zaliak travelled,
crossing one frontier after the next.

He tramped over deserts as wide as any,
hacked his way through cloud forests,
crossed rivers and seas.

And eventually one dusk,
he spied the outline of the
Slaked Grey Mountains.

Bedding down for the night, he stared up at the night sky and wondered whether the last stretch of the journey would bring the easy answer he so craved.

Then, as the first dawn light strained to warm the granite plain on which he had camped, Zaliak marched to the base of the most imposing mountain in the range.

A minute later, he was climbing.

Hour after hour, his boots clambered over the dull rock, his hands bloodied and his mind reeling from fatigue.

By the end of the first night, the young adventurer perceived he was only at the first stage, and that it might be many more days before he reached the Wise Man of Slew.

Again, he stared up at the starscape, wondering whether his journey was even valid at all.

The next morning, frozen to the bone,
Zaliak started climbing again…

Up, up, up…

Higher and higher.

Through the treeline and then zigzagging up through thistles and ferns.

After many days and nights of hardship,
he reached a valley.

Unlike any other he had encountered,
it was utterly silent, as though every insect,
bird, each individual creature, and even
the wind had been hushed.

Turning his ear to the distance, Zaliak listened.
Silence.

But then, the faintest wisp of sound…

A voice…

A voice that was speaking his name…

'Zaliak, hasten to the cave at the end of the valley, beyond the bamboo forest. Come, come, come… for I am waiting there for you.'

Intrigued and relieved, the young seeker quickened his step and found he had soon made his way through the bamboo forest.

Lost in the shadows beyond it,
there was indeed the mouth of a cave.

Approaching with care, Zaliak stepped forwards and peered into the cave.

A little time passed as his eyes grew accustomed to the darkness.

Gradually, he spied a shaft of blinding white light streaming from left to right at the back of the cave.

Caught in the dazzling rays was the shape of a man sitting cross-legged.

'Hello, Zaliak,' spoke the seated figure
as the fresh young adventurer approached.
'How do you know my name?' Zaliak asked.

'Because, as you have already grasped, I am the one known as the Wise Man of Slcw... and so, it is my prerogative to recognize simple matters such as your name, and far more difficult matters, too.'

Bowing his head in reverence, Zaliak breathed in, preparing to explain the nature of his quest. The wise man raised an index finger as if to silence the visitor.

'As you can imagine,' he said, 'I know full well why you are here. So, to save you time, I will provide the answer.'

'The answer…?'
'The answer to your dream.'

Zaliak flinched.
After travelling for so long, the youth had almost forgotten why he was where he was – in the valley at the top of the Slaked Grey Mountains.

'In my dream, every story in the world
was collected into a vast treasury,' he said,
the mumbled words echoing against the rock.

'That's right,' the sage said,
confirming the information.

‘So what am I to do?’ asked Zaliak.
The wise man shrugged.
‘Isn’t it obvious?’
‘No.’

'Well, think about it… a dream of astonishing importance in the dead of night… a night of the fullest moon for a thousand years.'

'Was it?'

'Yes, of course it was!'

'I *am* thinking about it... of my dream, and then of my journey through the cloud forests, across the rivers and the seas, up into the mountains, down this very valley... until I reached this exact spot.'

‘And what is it that you have perceived after all those adventures?’

Zaliak frowned.

'That I am supposed to devote my life to...'

'To what?'

The young man's brow furrowed like
a ploughed field ready for seeding.

‘Am I supposed to devote my life to collecting stories and tales?’ he asked.

The sage nodded.

‘Yes,’ he uttered, his tone more
certain than certainty itself.
‘How many stories am I to collect?’
‘Every story.’

‘*Every* story?!’

‘Yes! Every single one!’

‘Every story *where*?’

‘Every story ever spoken by a human tongue.’

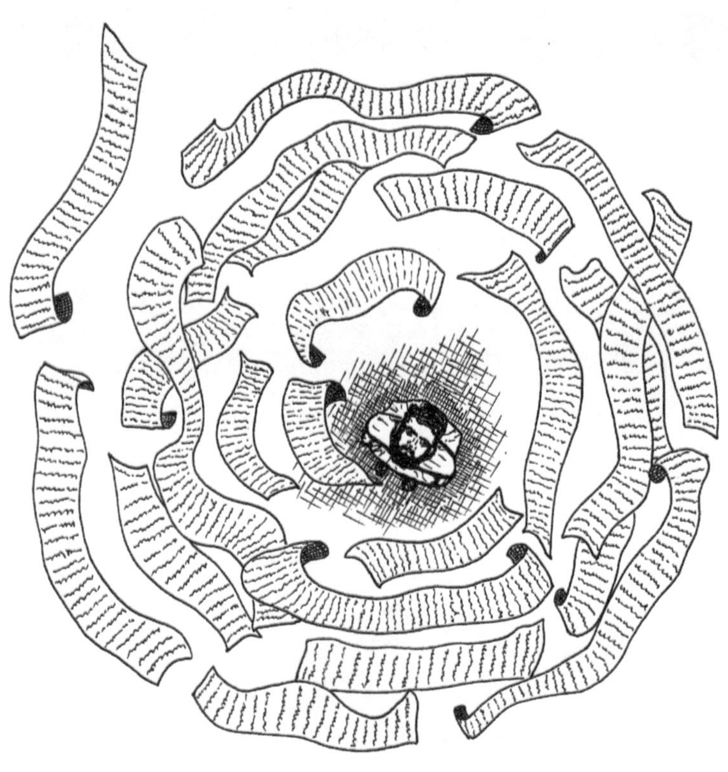

Zaliak gasped at the scope and scale of the project, his back warming with adrenalin. 'That will take months, or even years.'

‘It will take a lifetime,’ the sage corrected.

‘But… but… but… when I have collected the stories, what am I to do with them?’

The same index finger that had been held up into the shaft of light now pointed downwards and tapped the rock floor.

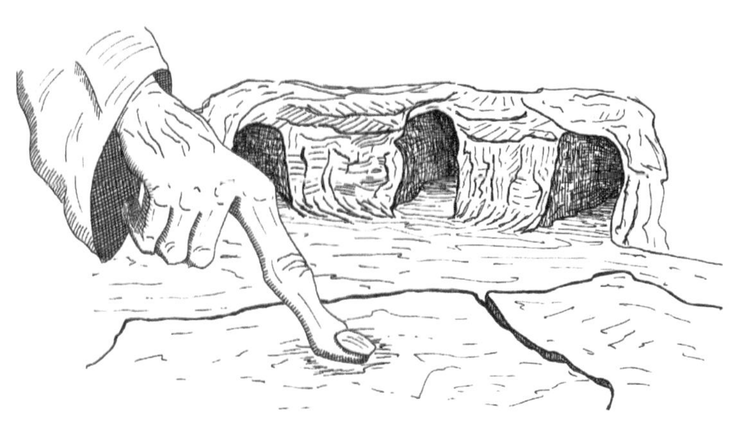

‘You’re to bring them here in batches,’ the wise man said, ‘and store them in the labyrinth of chambers that span out behind me.’

‘But how will I know when I have completed the task, and have deposited every single story ever told?’

The sage grinned.

'You will know because the Slaked Grey Mountains will shake and, as they shake, they will shimmer a ghostly shade of green.'

Zaliak was about to pose another question when the wise man clapped his hands twice.

'You'd better get going,' he said sharply. 'After all, you have a lot of work to do!'

So, following orders – orders shaped by a journey born in a dream – the youth set off in search of stories, tales, fables, and anecdotes.

Through days, weeks, months,
and years, he collected them.

Stories from the deepest recesses of the jungle.

From the frozen tundra of the Arctic, and the Antarctic.

From the snow-capped
peaks of the Himalayas.

From the centre of the Sahara,
and from the sands of the Gobi Desert.

From the forests of Siberia.

From the streets of every capital,
hamlet, and homestead on earth.

From the underground
cities of Cappadocia.

From people who spoke in
half-forgotten dialects.

From others whose worlds
were built on ancient tales.

From cultures in which stories were
little more than an amusement.

And from lands whose stories
were reflections of the tales.

Each year, Zaliak would travel to the caverns of the Slaked Grey Mountains, and place the stories he had collected in niches there.

As he returned over and over, assembling the repository, the young man – who was no longer so young or so raw as he had once been – came to understand that the niches were waiting for the stories he brought.

As soon as a fresh batch of tales was offloaded, the stories were sucked into place.

Decades passed.

And as they did so, Zaliak
became ripened by adventure.

From time to time he would reflect on
how young and foolish he had once been.
But, as he saw it, he was no less ripened now
than one of the characters in the tales he was
collecting and carrying year after year up into
the Slaked Grey Mountains.

Every year, when he deposited stories into the treasury, Zaliak tried to strike up a conversation with the Wise Man of Slew.

But as the years passed – and so many did pass – the sage seemed more and more reluctant to engage in conversation.

Indeed, it was as though with every new sheaf of tales, he was a little less willing to speak.

One year, when Zaliak appeared at the cave's mouth, he was so wizened with age that he could hardly give greeting.

'This is the last time I shall be making the journey here,' he said, the words burning his throat. 'You see, I have the very last bundle of tales from the farthest reaches of our mortal world.'

The wise man expressed a greeting. Unlike the adventurer, he appeared not to have aged at all in the decades since their first encounter.

'As a youth,' Zaliak said, pausing to summon his strength, 'I was filled head to toe with enthusiasm… a burning enthusiasm to see the Slaked Mountains shake and shimmer in a ghostly shade of green.

‘Nothing mattered so much to me as witnessing that sight. But now, with so many adventures to my name, I doubt that such a fanciful marvel could ever take place, even if every tale ever spoken were gathered here.’

Opening up his pack, Zaliak pulled out the last sheaf of stories and stuffed them into the niches, where millions of stories already lay.

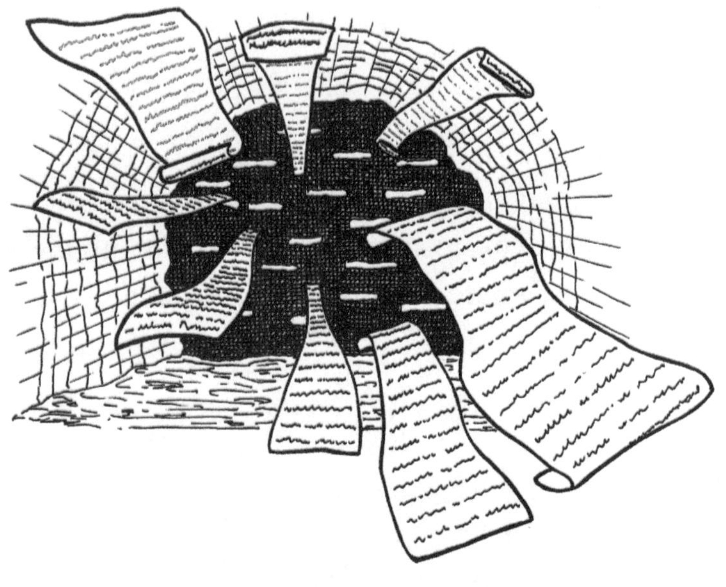

'There!' he exclaimed. 'That's it! That's every single story, tale, fable, and blessed anecdote, all collected together in the treasury.'

The sage managed half a smile.

'If that's it,' he said softly, 'why are the Slaked Grey Mountains not shaking and quaking, or shimmering with green ghostly light?'

The adventurer paused, a veil of discontent descending over his face. 'But I have not failed,' he whispered.

‘I am sure you have not.’

‘I have checked and double checked,’ Zaliak intoned, ‘and no tale remains unrecorded. Every single one has been set down and placed in this vault.’

The Wise Man of Slew drew
breath, and let out a sigh.
'Think,' he said.
'*Think*? Think *what*?'
'Think about your predicament.'

Rather than rising to the bait,
Zaliak calmed himself, and he thought.

He thought of all the mouths that had imparted stories in every corner of the world.

He thought of princes and queens…

Of warriors and knights…

Of carpenters and madmen…

Of witches and harlequins…

Of prisoners, farmers, scientists, fugitives,
and rogues… all of whom had provided tales.

As he considered them one by one,
a stray thought slipped onto the
stage of his mind.

A stray thought that seeded
itself and took root.

‘My God,’ Zaliak mumbled. ‘I know why the Slaked Grey Mountains have not shimmered, shaken, or quaked.’

Sitting cross-legged in the dazzling shaft of light, the wise man blinked.

‘The last story,’ he said.

Wheezing with age, the adventurer rummaged in his pack, pulling out a paper and pen. Then, taking his time, he wrote out the one story that was more important to him than any other.

The tale of his own life and adventures…

Adventures through which he had collected
every single story known to man.

As the final word was written in ink,
the Slaked Grey Mountains began to
tremble, shake, and quake.

And as they did so, the rock glowed
a ghostly shade of green.

Jubilantly, Zaliak rolled the last story up into a scroll and stuffed it in the niche awaiting it.

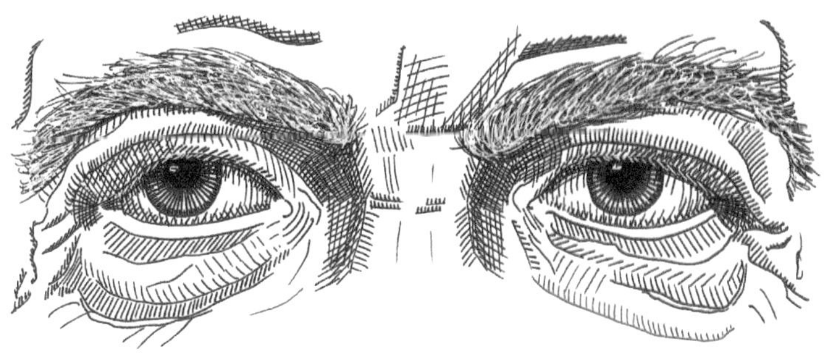

Then, bidding the Wise Man of Slew farewell, he turned on his heel and began the long journey home.

Finis

About the Author

Descended from a long line of storytellers, writers, and savants, Tahir Shah is one of the most prolific authors of his generation. He has published more than sixty books in numerous genres, including travel, fiction, and fantasy, as well as tales for children.

Raised in the tradition of Eastern 'teaching stories', Shah is passionate about stories and storytelling. He regards the ability to learn from folklore as being in us all, what he calls a 'default setting of humankind'. As well as having written scores of books, Shah has made documentaries for National Geographic TV and The History Channel. He is the founder and CEO of the charity, The Scheherazade Foundation.

About the Artist

Yaroslava Morosova is a self-taught artist from Ukraine, now based in the UK. After years working in the field of transportation, she redirected her life and work towards art and storytelling. Through study, practice, and experimentation, Yaroslava now works full-time using her creative expression to produce, in her words, 'a rich fantasy world, the perfection of which has no limit'.

Books By Tahir Shah

Travel

Trail of Feathers
Travels With Myself
Beyond the Devil's Teeth
In Search of King Solomon's Mines
House of the Tiger King
In Arabian Nights
The Caliph's House
Sorcerer's Apprentice
Journey Through Namibia

Novels

Jinn Hunter: Book One – The Prism
Jinn Hunter: Book Two – The Jinnslayer
Jinn Hunter: Book Three – The Perplexity
Hannibal Fogg and the Supreme Secret of Man
Hannibal Fogg and the Codex Cartographica
Casablanca Blues
Eye Spy
Godman
Paris Syndrome
Timbuctoo

Nasrudin

Travels With Nasrudin
The Misadventures of the Mystifying Nasrudin
The Peregrinations of the Perplexing Nasrudin
The Voyages and Vicissitudes of Nasrudin
Nasrudin in the Land of Fools

Teaching Stories

The Arabian Nights Adventures

Scorpion Soup

Tales Told to a Melon

The Afghan Notebook

The Caravanserai Stories

Ghoul Brothers

Hourglass

Imaginist

Jinn's Treasure

Jinnlore

Mellified Man

Skeleton Island

Wellspring

When the Sun Forgot to Rise

Outrunning the Reaper

The Cap of Invisibility

On Backgammon Time

The Wondrous Seed

The Paradise Tree

Mouse House

The Hoopoe's Flight

The Old Wind

A Treasury of Tales

Daydreams of an Octopus & Other Stories

Miscellaneous

The Reason to Write

Zigzag Think

Being Myself

Research

Cultural Research

The Middle East Bedside Book

Three Essays

Anthologies

The Anthologies

The Clockmaker's Box

The Tahir Shah Fiction Reader

The Tahir Shah Travel Reader

Edited by

Congress With a Crocodile

A Son of a Son, Volume I

A Son of a Son, Volume II

Screenplays

Casablanca Blues: The Screenplay

Timbuctoo: The Screenplay

A REQUEST

If you enjoyed this book, please review it on your favourite online retailer or review website.

Reviews are an author's best friend.

To stay in touch with Tahir Shah, and to hear about his upcoming releases before anyone else, please sign up for his mailing list:

 http://tahirshah.com/newsletter

And to follow him on social media, please go to any of the following links:

 http://www.twitter.com/humanstew

 @tahirshah999

 http://www.facebook.com/TahirShahAuthor

 http://www.youtube.com/user/tahirshah999

 http://www.pinterest.com/tahirshah

 https://www.goodreads.com/tahirshahauthor

http://www.tahirshah.com

www.ingramcontent.com/pod-product-compliance
Lightning Source LLC
Chambersburg PA
CBHW030521310726
48979CB00010B/1758/J

* 9 7 8 1 9 1 4 9 6 0 8 8 8 *